W9-AAE-087

MICHELLE
KWAN

(Photo on front cover)

Michelle Kwan performs her routine in the women's short program at the World Figure Skating Championships in Edmonton, Canada in March of 1996.

(Photo on previous pages)

Kwan runs through part of her routine while posing for promotional photos.

Printed in the United States of America.

Photography: Wide World Photos, Inc.

Library of Congress Cataloging-in-Publication Data
Rambeck, Richard.
Michelle Kwan / by Richard Rambeck.
p. cm.
Summary: A biography of world champion figure skater whose goal is to win gold medals in the 1998, 2002, and 2006 Winter Olympics.
ISBN 1-56766-461-X (smythe-sewn library bound)

1. Kwan, Michelle, 1980- — Juvenile literature. 2. Women skaters — United States — Biography — Juvenile literature. [1. Kwan, Michelle, 1980- . 2. Ice skaters. 3. Chinese Americans — Biography. 4. Women — Biography.] I. Title.

GV850.K93R36 1998 97-12956
796.91'2'092 — dc21 CIP
[B] AC

MICHELLE
KWAN

BY RICHARD RAMBECK

Kwan went into the lead in Paris, France in November of 1996, with this women's short program performance.

Her goal is right there, above the dresser in her bedroom. One word on the the giant sticker says it all: Nagano. For U.S. ice skater Michelle Kwan, Nagano is where she wants her dream to come true. Nagano is the city in Japan where the 1998 Winter Olympics will be held. Kwan wants to leave Nagano with something she won't bring to Japan: a gold medal in the women's figure skating event. She dreams about winning that medal almost every night. "In my dreams, I'm crying because I'm happy and I have the gold."

Then she wakes up — and immediately remembers why she needs to practice skating three hours a day, seven days a week. Every day, Kwan goes to the ice rink in Lake Arrowhead, California. Every day, she works on the jumps that helped make her the U.S. and world women's figure skating champion in 1996. Kwan was only 15 years old when she won both those titles. She was the youngest U.S. women's champion in 32 years. Kwan was also the third-youngest women's world champion in history. And her career was only getting started.

Kwan holds up her gold medal at the World Figure Skating Championships in Edmonton, Canada.

Kwan wants more than a gold medal in 1998. She also wants one in the 2002 Winter Olympics — and in the 2006 games, too. No one has ever won three women's figure skating gold medals. Kwan, who will be only 25 years old in 2006, thinks she has the ability to make history. And she just might. At the beginning of 1997, Kwan was clearly the best women's skater in the United States — and everywhere else. After winning the world title in 1996, Kwan was asked about the pressure of being Number 1. Pressure? What pressure? She doesn't think about being Number 1. She just thinks about skating.

Kwan performing a triple jump that earned her some perfect scores.

Kwan says that when she takes the ice in a world championship, it's just like being at home in California. "I try to go into a competition like it's another practice," she said. She proved that at the 1996 world championships in Edmonton, Alberta. Kwan was the leader after the short program. Her lead was surprising because Kwan was ahead of the 1995 world champion, Chen Lu of China. Chen, who was four years older than the 15-year-old Kwan, skated first in the long program. The Chinese woman turned in one of the greatest performances in history.

In her long program, Chan did six triple jumps. (In a triple jump, the skater spins completely around three times while in the air.) Two of the judges gave Chen a perfect score of 6.0. She had never had a 6.0 before. When Chen's scores were flashed on the scoreboard, Kwan was hiding in the flower-girls' room. She didn't want to see Chen's scores, but she could hear the stadium announcer call them out. "I thought, I'll have to do a quadruple toe loop (jump) to win," Kwan said. She was joking, but it didn't seem as if she had a chance to win.

Kwan in the spotlight at the Parade of Champions in Edmonton, Canada.

Kwan's coach, Frank Carroll, told her she did have a chance. Kwan believed him. "Then I got myself down to earth and said, 'Just go for it. Go for everything. Why not?'" Kwan recalled. She took the ice knowing that even one little mistake would keep her from being a world champion. But Kwan wasn't nervous. After all, this was just like practice, wasn't it? She just needed to have a perfect practice. Kwan performed as well as she ever had. Her program called for her to do six triple jumps. She did those jumps perfectly. No falls, no slips.

In the final seconds of her program, Kwan pulled a surprise move. She did an unplanned seventh triple jump. It was as good

Kwan placed first in the ladies' free skate at Skate America International '95.

as the other six. When Kwan's routine ended, the crowd let out a huge roar. Kwan at last acted like the 15-year-old she was. She started crying, just like in her dreams. "The emotions took over when I realized this was the world championships and I'd just skated the best I ever had in my life," Kwan said. But was this performance good enough for her to overtake Chen? It was. Kwan got perfect 6.0 scores from two judges and 5.9s from seven others.

The world had a new women's figure skating champion. "I never saw two performances like that in my life," Morry Stillwell of the U.S. Figure Skating Association said of Kwan and Chen. "For Michelle to add that jump in the last seconds, that's sport." Kwan became the third-youngest women's world champion in history. The two who were younger — Sonia Henie in 1927 and Oksana Baiul in 1993 — both went on to win Olympic gold medals later in their careers. Kwan also became the youngest U.S. skater to claim a women's world title. When she left Edmonton, Kwan knew there was only one honor left for her to win.

Michelle, left, and her sister Karen, who is also a figure skater, being interviewed after Michelle became the youngest woman in 32 years to win the U.S. Figure Skating Championship.

Michelle Kwan has dreamed of winning an Olympic gold medal for most of her life. Born on July 7, 1980, she was the youngest of Danny and Estella Kwan's three children. When Michelle was five, she went with her mother and sister Karen to watch brother Ron's hockey practice. Soon after, both Michelle and Karen said they wanted to skate, too. Within a year, Michelle entered and won her first figure skating competition. In 1988, Michelle watched the Winter Olympics on television. She saw U.S. skater Brian Boitano win the men's gold medal.

Kwan and her coach Frank Carroll react to her gold medal winning score at the World Figure Skating Championships.

Michelle Kwan wanted to do what Boitano had done — the next day. "I thought OK, tomorrow I'll go to the Olympics," Kwan said. It took longer than a day, of course, but Kwan nearly made it to the 1994 Winter Olympics in Lillehammer, Norway. Beginning in 1992, she rose quickly through the ranks of U.S. skaters. In 1992, Kwan finished ninth in the U.S. Junior Nationals. Her coach, Frank Carroll, felt Kwan needed at least another two years of competing with the juniors. Kwan had other ideas. One year after placing ninth in the U.S. Juniors, Kwan wound up sixth in the 1993 U.S. Senior Nationals.

Kwan also won the 1993 U.S. Olympic Festival as well as the 1994 World Junior Championships. In the 1994 U.S. Senior Nationals, she finished second. That normally would have earned her a place on the Olympic team. However, Nancy Kerrigan, who was injured and unable to compete in the Nationals, was given one of the two U.S. Olympic spots. Kwan did go to Norway for the Olympics, but as an alternate. "I never really got to see the ice rink (in Norway)" Kwan said. "I never got to see the Olympic Village. It wasn't really much of an Olympic experience."

Kwan thanks the audience for their cheers after her performance in Springfield, Massachusetts in November of 1996.

Kwan's career really took off in 1995. Early in the year, she finished second at the U.S. Senior Nationals and then fourth at the world championships. In the spring, she was given a chance to go on tour with Brian Boitano and other ice skating greats. Carroll urged Kwan to go. He thought it would be an excellent chance for her to see what it took to be a champion. "Great skating breeds great skating," he told Kwan. When she returned from the tour, Kwan started winning competitions. She finished first at both the 1995 Skate America and Skate Canada events.

Kwan shows beauty and grace during the women's free program at Tokyo, Japan's Olympic Gymnasium in January of 1997.

Kwan had literally grown up. When she first started skating in senior events, she was 4-foot-9 and weighed only 77 pounds. When she won the 1996 U.S. senior title, Kwan was 5-foot-2 and 98 pounds. She skated to the top of the world rankings in 1996, but she soon found out how hard it is to stay Number 1. At the 1997 U.S. Senior Nationals, she took the lead after the short program. But then Kwan fell three times during her long program. She lost her title to 14-year-old Tara Lipinski. Even though Kwan finished second, she hadn't forgotten her main goal. It was right there on a giant sticker above her dresser: Nagano, Olympic gold in 1998.